For Raymond,
brightest and best

First published 1994 by
Walker Books Ltd, 87 Vauxhall Walk
London SE11 5HJ

2 4 6 8 10 9 7 5 3 1

This book has been typeset in Garamond.

Printed in Hong Kong

British Library Cataloguing in Publication Data
A catalogue record for this book is
available from the British Library.

ISBN 0-7445-2577-2

HUMPHREY THUD

Camilla Ashforth

WALKER BOOKS
LONDON

Horatio had learnt a disappearing trick.

"One,

two,

three...

hoopla!" he called, and jumped
into his sock.

"Can I do that?" someone asked.

It was Humphrey Thud.
"It's easy," said Horatio. "You just say the magic word and jump into the sock. Let's show James."

James was by his Useful Box,
wondering what to draw.
"Can we show you our magic trick?"
asked Horatio. "Humphrey can
disappear."

Humphrey charged towards the sock.
"Hoopla!" cried Horatio.

THUD!

"Have I disappeared?" Humphrey asked.

"Some of you has,"
said James.

"I must have said the wrong magic word," said Horatio.

James had an idea. "That sock's too small for an elephant," he said. "I have something bigger in my Useful Box."

James took out a flag and gave it
to Horatio.
"One, two, three … hoopla!"
Horatio called. He threw
the flag over
Humphrey.

A lot of Humphrey didn't disappear.

"Maybe Humphrey's just too big,"
said James. "Why don't you make
his hat disappear instead?"

When Horatio came back, he
couldn't see the hat anywhere.
"It's disappeared," he cried.

"Hooray!" shouted Humphrey.

James was worried. He hoped the
hat wasn't in his Useful Box.
He opened the lid and looked inside.

James rummaged in his Useful Box.
Humphrey waited.
"This is my best cow," James said.

Humphrey was really missing his hat.

"Can I have my hat back now?"
he asked.

Oh dear, thought Horatio.

Horatio tried to think of a magic
word to bring back Humphrey's hat.

"Bee!

Button!

Bumble!

BOO!" he cried.

But Humphrey's hat didn't come back.

"James could lend you something like this," said Horatio. "Maybe."

But James had forgotten all about
Humphrey's hat and was sorting
out his Useful Bits.

"Humbugs!" he said. "I've found
my humbugs."

Humphrey stood up and stretched his trunk towards James. "Could I have a humbug?" he asked. "I like humbugs."

"Humbugs!" cried Horatio. "That's the magic word. Look, Humphrey's hat came back!"

Humphrey put on his hat and
took Horatio for a ride.
James sat down to draw.

"Here are my two best friends," said
James. "Now let's all have a humbug."